KV-437-494

# Let's have a
# SLEEPOVER

This book belongs to

.................................................................

# Let's have a sleepover

A LAUGHING LOBSTER BOOK 978-1-914564-33-8

Published in Great Britain by Laughing Lobster, an imprint of Centum Publishing Ltd.
This edition published 2022.

1 3 5 7 9 10 8 6 4 2

Illustrations by Sue Mason.

Laughing Lobster, an imprint of Centum Publishing Ltd, 20 Devon Square, Newton Abbot, Devon, TQ12 2HR, UK. 9/10 Fenian St, Dublin 2, D02 RX24, Ireland.

books@centumpublishingltd.co.uk

LAUGHING LOBSTER, CENTUM PUBLISHING LIMITED Reg. No. 08497203

A CIP catalogue record for this book is available from the British Library.

Printed in China.

# Meet the characters...

Hello, I'm **Alice.**

And I'm **Joe.** We're both going to sleepovers.

I'm going to stay at **Mia's** house with **Poppy.** I can't wait!

And I'm staying next door at **Noah's** house with **Tom.** It's going to be so much fun!

(We all live on **ACORN STREET!**)

Something very exciting is happening this weekend – I'm going to my first sleepover.
Poppy and I are going to play at Mia's house and then when it gets dark we're not going home. We're going to stay for the whole night!

Mia's sleepover sounded like so much fun that we wanted one too! Noah's mum said that Tom and I could stay at their house. We're going to sleep in Noah's living room. It's so cool because we get to make our own beds and sleep on the floor!

At the end of school, we all talk about our sleepovers.
"Maybe I'll ask Mum if we can sleep in a blanket fort," says Mia.
"*Our* sleepover is going to be the best sleepover EVER," shouts Poppy,
just as Joe, Noah and Tom walk by.

"No it's not," says Noah. "OUR sleepover is going to be lots **more fun** than yours!"

"No, OUR sleepover is going to be even more fun than birthdays," I tell the boys.

"Well ours will be **more fun** than Christmas!" says Tom.

Everybody thinks that their sleepover will be more fun . . . but I know ours will be the BEST!

"Alice, there's lots to get ready for your first sleepover. Shall we write a list?" says Mum.
So I get out my favourite pen and some paper to write a list to help me remember all the things I need.

Must have:
Pyjamas
Toothbrush
**Must, must have:**
My pony, Buttons
My sleepover bed

"Joe, remember you can come back home, even if it's in the middle of the night," says Mum. She's packed me a rucksack full of night-time things.

"Mum, it's going to be **SOOOO** much fun! Why would I come home early?" I ask her.

But she just keeps giving me lots of big hugs and kisses.

"Hi, Alice!" shouts Mia as she and her mum open the front door.
Poppy is already there and we all run inside to start our sleepover.

"Do you like my new super hero costume, Joe?" asks Tom when we arrive at Noah's front door. We both knock as loud as we can. Mum gives me another big kiss.
"I'm only next door if you need me," she tells me.

Now the sleepover can begin! Mia takes us to her bedroom. She has lots of treasures from her holidays, there are things from all over the world. Mia's bedroom is so much bigger than mine.

On the floor there are two beds made for Poppy and me. But that means I won't get to use my new sleepover bed.
"I have a special sleepover bed to sleep in," I tell Mia. I pull it out of the bag and show the others. "It already has a blanket and a pillow stuck to it!"
"That's brilliant!" she says.
"I want one of those for our next sleepover," grins Poppy.

"I've got a great idea," says Noah. "We need to make a secret password!" he shouts.
"Password?" I say. I don't understand what he means.
"Yes, a secret password for our sleepover club! You can't tell anyone else the password," Noah tells us.
It takes a long time, but in the end we decide that the password is 'super hero'.

The last time I came around to play at Noah's the lounge looked different – the furniture has been moved to make space for our beds.

Mia's mum has made us a special sleepover tea – we're having pizza!
We all sit round the table and Mia shows us how to make long,
stretchy strings of cheese from our pizza.
"We don't do this at home," I giggle.

After tea, Noah's stepdad Andy puts on a film for us to watch.
We all sit on our beds and eat popcorn!
"Tonight is a real adventure," says Tom.
"Yeah, I've never slept on the floor before!" I tell them.

"Time to brush your teeth," Mia's Mum tells us.
"It's funny to brush my teeth in somebody else's bathroom,"
smiles Poppy.
I've only brushed my teeth in my house before too. When I think
about home my tummy feels a bit funny.

We get into our different beds and I snuggle Buttons. My bedroom
feels very far away now.

"Let's tell each other our favourite stories," suggests Poppy.

Mia goes first. "Once upon a time . . ."

After we've brushed our teeth my bed has gone flat.
"Never mind," says Andy and he puts some of the sofa cushions
on the floor for me to sleep on instead. They're not very comfy
and I wish that I could sleep in my own bed.

The street looks different through Noah's windows. The trees
make scary shadows on the walls. Is it my imagination or are
the shadows getting bigger?
"I'll close the curtains," Andy says.
"We need them open so that we can look for shooting stars," says Noah.
I'd like the curtain to be closed, but I don't want to mess up Noah's
plans, so I don't say anything.

". . . and they all lived happily ever after."
"I'm sleepy," yawns Poppy.
It's really late now and I'm not sure that I want to stay at Mia's house anymore. "I miss my Mum," I tell Mia.

Mia tries to think of things to make me happy. "Would you like my prettiest shell, or my favourite fairy costume, or a cuddle of Sydney?" she asks.

"No it's OK, I have Buttons to cuddle," I tell her. But the person I really want to cuddle is my mum.

"I know what will work!" says Mia.
Mia asks her mum if I can use the telephone to call Mum and Dad.
I tell them goodnight and Mum says that I will see her in the morning.
Mia was right, I feel much better now.

We run back up the stairs to Mia's room. Poppy has fallen asleep! So Mia and I snuggle into her bed again and tell each other more stories.

"Now I've seen three shooting stars!" says Tom.
Suddenly I see a huge wavy monster with massive branchy arms.
"What was that?" I shout and hide under my duvet.

"It's only the tree outside," says Noah.
"There are some funny shadows and noises in your house," I say
to Noah.
"Would you like to borrow my special pillow? It always helps me,"
Tom asks me.
"No thanks," I say. I want to be back in my bedroom
now. I'm used to the shadows in there.

Noah says he's had a brilliant idea and he runs out of the living room.
I hope his idea is brilliant because I'm not so sure I like sleepovers.

Then Noah bursts round the corner with the night-light from his bedroom. It looks just like a rocket.

"Cool, now I can see everything," I say.

The shadows don't look scary with Noah's night-light so we can all look for more shooting stars.

It's exciting to wake up in Mia's bedroom. Dudley comes in and bounces on us . . .

. . . and then we all have pancakes for breakfast. Pancakes are my favourite breakfast of all!

In the morning we jump all around Noah's living room.
"Sleepovers are the biggest adventures ever!" I shout.
"They're even better than seeing shooting stars," laughs Tom.

After Noah's mum has made us breakfast, it's time for everyone
to go home. Alice and Poppy are leaving Mia's house too.
Alice and I agree that both our sleepovers were the most fun.
"Next time I want to camp in tents," I tell Alice.
"I want another sleepover tonight," she grins.